Brave
Squish Rabbit

Katherine Battersby

VIKING
An Imprint of Penguin Group (USA) Inc.

Squish was just a little rabbit.
But being little led to big fears.

Squish was scared of many things.

Like storms.

And chickens.

And especially the dark.
The dark was so big, it was everywhere.

Squish tried to hide from the dark.

But wherever he went,
it followed.

Playing with his friend Twitch
helped Squish forget his fears.

One day, Squish went to meet
Twitch at their secret tree house.
But when he arrived, Twitch was gone.

She'd left a note,
but Squish couldn't read it.

Outside, it got darker and darker.

Inside, Squish got scared
and goosebumply.

Squish worried Twitch was trapped

. . . in the dark

. . . in a storm

. . . with a chicken.

There was only one thing to do.

Squish prepared for

the worst . . .

And stepped into the dark.

Finally Squish saw something.
It wasn't storms or chickens like he'd feared.

It was a bit dark . . . .

but not at all scary.

Squish was just a little rabbit,
but being brave made him feel much bigger.

For Julie,
my friend and writing partner in crime,
who laughs at the right moments

VIKING

Published by the Penguin Group

Penguin Young Readers Group, 345 Hudson Street, New York, New York 10014, U.S.A.

Penguin Group (Canada), 90 Eglinton Avenue East, Suite 700, Toronto, Ontario, Canada M4P 2Y3

(a division of Pearson Penguin Canada Inc.)

Penguin Books Ltd, 80 Strand, London WC2R 0RL, England

Penguin Ireland, 25 St Stephen's Green, Dublin 2, Ireland (a division of Penguin Books Ltd)

Penguin Group (Australia), 250 Camberwell Road, Camberwell, Victoria 3124, Australia

(a division of Pearson Australia Group Pty Ltd)

Penguin Books India Pvt Ltd, 11 Community Centre, Panchsheel Park, New Delhi – 110 017, India

Penguin Group (NZ), 67 Apollo Drive, Rosedale, Auckland 0632, New Zealand (a division of Pearson New Zealand Ltd.)

Penguin Books (South Africa) (Pty) Ltd, 24 Sturdee Avenue, Rosebank, Johannesburg 2196, South Africa

Penguin Books Ltd, Registered Offices: 80 Strand, London WC2R 0RL, England

First published in the United States of America by Viking, a division of Penguin Young Readers Group, 2012

1   3   5   7   9   10   8   6   4   2

LIBRARY OF CONGRESS CATALOGING-IN-PUBLICATION DATA
Battersby, Katherine.
Brave Squish Rabbit / by Katherine Battersby.
p. cm.
Summary: Squish, a little rabbit who is afraid of nearly everything, ventures into the night during a storm to find his friend,
Twitch, who he fears may have encountered chickens.
ISBN 978-0-670-01268-8 (hardcover)
[1. Rabbits—Fiction. 2. Fear of the dark—Fiction. 3. Courage—Fiction. 4. Friendship—Fiction.] I. Title.
PZ7.B324376Br 2012
[E]—dc23
2011048415

Manufactured in China   Set in Cochin Medium
The illustrations for this book are a collage of ink, watercolor, textiles, and digital manipulation.

ALWAYS LEARNING   PEARSON